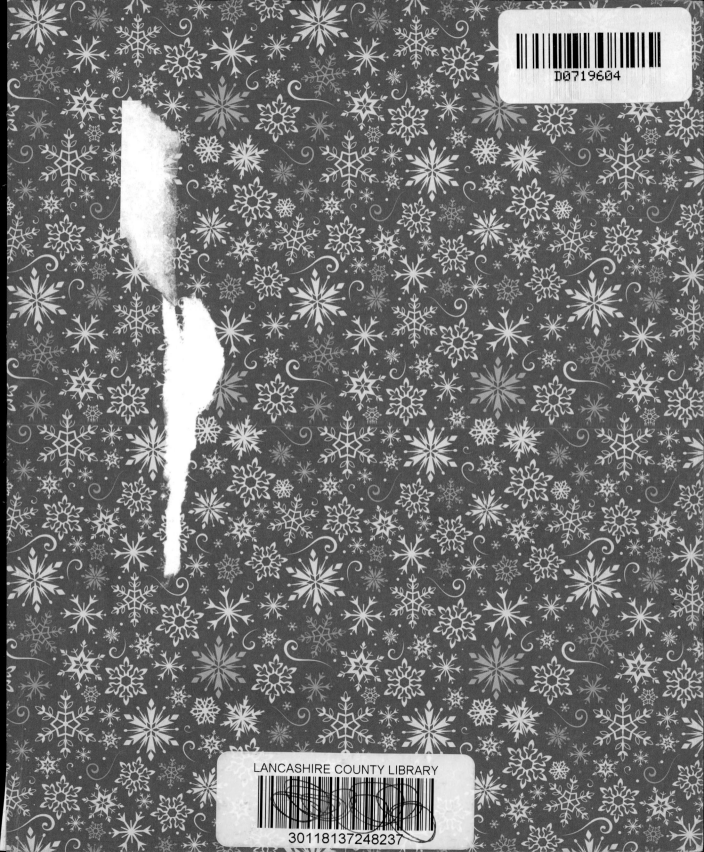

STORYTIME COLLECTION

STORYTIME COLLECTION

This book belongs to

_____

_____

Autumn
Publishing

Published in 2018
by Autumn Publishing
Cottage Farm
Sywell
NN6 0BJ
www.igloobooks.com

GUA009 0718
2 4 6 8 10 9 7 5 3
ISBN 978-1-78810-817-1

Printed and manufactured in China

From the Movie

Disney

FROZEN

✳ STORYTIME COLLECTION ✳

STORYTIME COLLECTION · STORYTIME COLLECTION

The kingdom of Arendelle was a happy and beautiful place. Nestled amongst the mountains and fjords of the far north, the townsfolk lived in peace and harmony. However, their king and queen lived with a secret worry.

Their eldest daughter, Elsa, had a magical power.
She could freeze things and was able to create snow
and ice with her hands!

Anna, the king and queen's younger daughter, adored
her sister and always wanted to play with her.

Unknown to their parents, the two would often play in the winter wonderlands created by Elsa. There were snow slides and frozen floors they could ice-skate on.

Elsa even created a snowman, called Olaf, who would play with them both.

On one such night, Elsa accidentally hit Anna in the head with a blast of icy magic. The little girl fell to the ground and a white streak appeared in her hair. "Mama! Papa!" cried Elsa, who was upset she had hurt her sister.

Knowing of only one way to save Anna, the king
and queen rushed to the land of the trolls, who they
knew had magical healing powers. A wise old troll,
Grand Pabbie, made Anna better, but in doing so,
had to remove her memories of Elsa's magic.

He also warned that Elsa's magic would only grow
stronger. "You must learn to control it," he said to
Elsa, who was frightened by the power she possessed.
Grand Pabbie then turned to the king and queen.
"Fear will be her enemy," he told them.

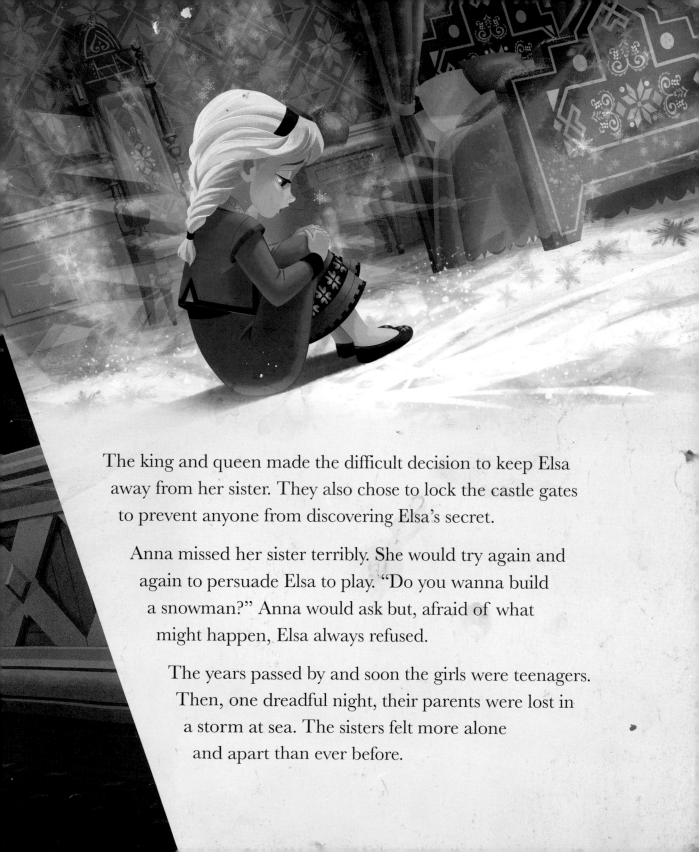

The king and queen made the difficult decision to keep Elsa away from her sister. They also chose to lock the castle gates to prevent anyone from discovering Elsa's secret.

Anna missed her sister terribly. She would try again and again to persuade Elsa to play. "Do you wanna build a snowman?" Anna would ask but, afraid of what might happen, Elsa always refused.

The years passed by and soon the girls were teenagers. Then, one dreadful night, their parents were lost in a storm at sea. The sisters felt more alone and apart than ever before.

Elsa soon came of age, and so, it was her duty to become queen of Arendelle. On a beautiful summer's day, when the sky was bluer than it had ever been, the gates, for one day only, would be opened to celebrate the coronation. Anna was very excited at the chance to meet new people.

Meanwhile, Elsa was worrying about the coronation.
What if her magic was discovered? What would people say?
As she practised for the ceremony, she found herself struggling
to control her powers. Would she be able to contain them
when the time came?

Outside, Anna had met a handsome prince.
He had accidentally bumped into her with
his horse, but Anna was so captivated by his
charm that she soon forgave him.

He introduced himself as Prince Hans of the Southern Isles. "I'd like to formally apologise for hitting the Princess of Arendelle with my horse," he added.

"No, no it's fine," replied Anna, awkwardly. It was clear to see, the pair were already very fond of each other.

It was soon time for the coronation. Elsa slowly removed her gloves and picked up the royal orb and sceptre.

Despite her best efforts, they slowly began to freeze. Luckily, the ceremony was completed just in time. She was now Queen Elsa of Arendelle.

All the while, Anna stood by Elsa's side, sneaking glances at Hans.

At the Coronation Ball, Anna and Hans spent
every moment together, laughing and enjoying each
other's company. It was love at first sight,
so they decided to get engaged!

Anna excitedly took Hans to introduce him to Elsa
and tell her sister of their happy news. Elsa was very
surprised. "You can't marry a man you just met,"
she said.

"You can if it's true love," insisted Anna.

"No!" cried Elsa, firmly. She would not allow Anna and Hans to marry. Having had enough of her sister, Elsa tried to leave.

"No, wait!" cried Anna, who grabbed Elsa's hand and accidentally pulled her glove off. "I can't live like this any more," she added. "Why do you shut me out?"

"Enough!" cried Elsa. With her hand exposed, she was unable to control herself and released a sea of ice across the ballroom. Everyone stared in disbelief.

Elsa ran from the kingdom, unknowingly turning it from a warm summer's day to a cold land of ice. Believing her problems were behind her, she headed high into the mountains.

No longer having to hide her magical powers, she created stunning ice sculptures, a beautiful ice palace and even the same snowman she had made when she was younger.

Elsa even transformed the way she looked. She magically removed her crown and royal clothing and replaced them with a beautiful, glittering ice-blue dress.

She may have been alone, but she was happy and felt free for the first time since she could remember.

Anna, meanwhile, was desperate to find her sister. Not only to make sure she was okay, but also so she could get her to unfreeze the kingdom.

So, leaving Hans in charge of Arendelle, Anna rode away on a horse and headed to the mountains.

As Anna journeyed further towards the mountains, the weather became worse. Frightened by a gathering storm, Anna's horse threw her off and bolted back to Arendelle, leaving her alone in the snow.

She brushed herself off and continued on foot. The further she went, the colder she became but, luckily, she spotted a small building ahead.

The small building turned out to be a trading post. Inside, Anna gathered up a pair of winter boots and warm clothing. Then, a young man named Kristoff trudged in.

He was an ice harvester and complained about a snowstorm from the North Mountain that was ruining his business. After all, no one needed to buy ice when they were surrounded by it!

"North Mountain," said Anna to herself, knowing this must be where Elsa had gone to. She looked at Kristoff. "I want you to take me to the North Mountain," she said. "I know how to stop this winter."

Kristoff reluctantly agreed to help. He needed the snow to go, so his ice harvester business would pick up again.

As Kristoff and his reindeer friend, Sven, led Anna up to the summit of the North Mountain, she was stunned by what she saw. "I never knew winter could be so... beautiful," she said.

Suddenly, a voice spoke from behind them. "But it's so white," it said. "How about a little colour?" Anna, Kristoff and Sven spun around. Behind them was a living snowman! "I'm Olaf," he said.

Anna recognised him from when she was younger.
"Do you know where Elsa is?" asked Anna. Olaf said he did.
In fact, that's where he'd travelled from, but he wanted
to know why they needed to find her.

"We need her to bring back summer," added Kristoff. Olaf
loved the idea of summer, so happily helped them to find Elsa.

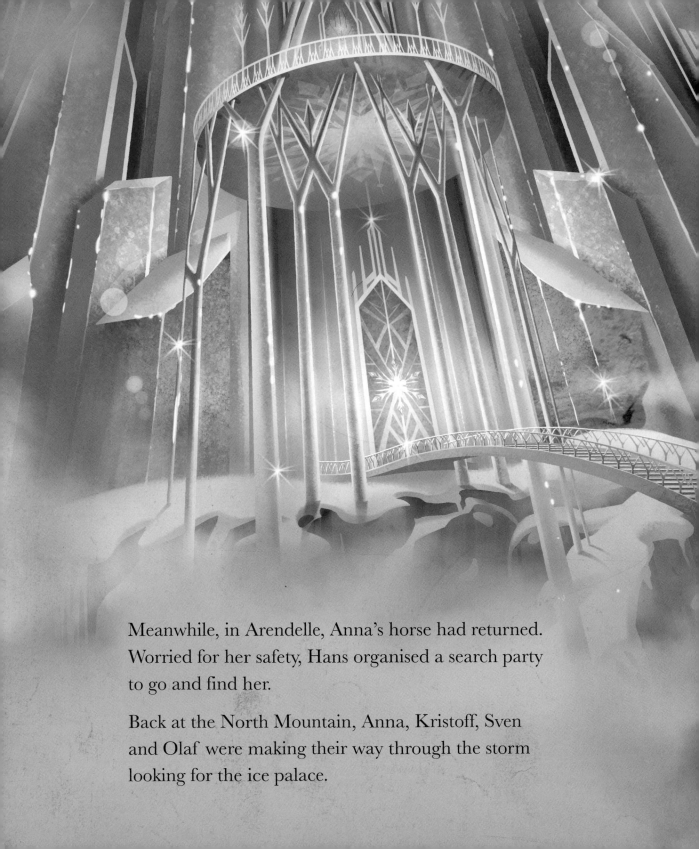

Meanwhile, in Arendelle, Anna's horse had returned. Worried for her safety, Hans organised a search party to go and find her.

Back at the North Mountain, Anna, Kristoff, Sven and Olaf were making their way through the storm looking for the ice palace.

Moments later, Olaf said, "I found a staircase that leads exactly to where you want to go."

Anna followed Olaf up the ice staircase. The palace was breathtaking!

Anna was excited to have found her sister, but Elsa wasn't. "You should probably go," she said, afraid she may hurt Anna again.

But Anna wouldn't leave. She wanted her sister to come back home, where she belonged, and to unfreeze Arendelle. "You set off an eternal winter," added Anna.

Elsa began to feel frightened. She couldn't unfreeze Arendelle. She didn't know how to. "Sure you can," said Anna, who moved closer to her sister.

As she did so, however, Elsa, unable to control her fear, released a burst of icy snowflakes, one of which hit her sister in the heart.

Kristoff, who had followed Anna into the palace, rushed towards her. "I think we should go," he said.

"No!" cried Anna. "I'm not leaving without you, Elsa!"

"Yes, you are," replied her sister. Then, Elsa conjured up a giant snow monster who threw Anna, Kristoff and Olaf out of the palace and off the North Mountain.

At the bottom of the mountain, Kristoff noticed Anna's hair had started to turn white. "Anna, you need help," he said. Kristoff explained he knew someone who could help, so they headed off to find them.

Soon after Kristoff had led everyone away from the
North Mountain, Hans arrived with the search party.
They were greeted by the snow monster who, wanting
to keep Elsa safe, blocked their way.

However, the mob would not be so easily put off,
and they attacked the giant, frozen beast.

As night fell, Kristoff led Anna, Sven and Olaf into a rocky valley. It was here where they met his friends, the trolls. They were like family to Kristoff, having raised him since he was a boy.

The trolls were very excited to meet Anna and, not realising she loved Hans, thought the princess was a great match for Kristoff. However, they could see that she wasn't well and so called for their leader, Grand Pabbie.

Grand Pabbie quickly realised what was wrong with Anna, however, unlike when she was a child, he was unable to help. There was ice in her heart and it would freeze her solid within a day. However, there was still hope. "An act of true love can thaw a frozen heart," said Grand Pabbie.

With time running out, Kristoff, with Olaf and Sven's help, decided to take Anna back to Arendelle. Surely a true love's kiss from Prince Hans would be able to break the spell and save Anna.

Back at the ice palace, some of the search party had made it past the snow monster and attacked Elsa. Using her powers, she pinned one of the men against the wall with shards of ice. Suddenly, Hans ran in. "Queen Elsa!" he cried. "Don't be the monster they think you are."

Realising what she had done, Elsa released the man. Moments later, another man fired a crossbow at her. Hans pushed it aside just in time. However, the arrow hit a chandelier, which fell to the floor, knocking the queen unconscious.

A few hours later, Elsa slowly opened her eyes. Her hands were in iron shackles and she was locked in a prison cell. She walked over to the window and saw she was back in Arendelle, but was shocked to see what her powers had done to her kingdom. Just then, Prince Hans entered the cell. "Why did you bring me here?" asked Elsa.

"I couldn't just let them kill you," replied Hans. She asked him to fetch Anna, but on hearing she had yet to return, Elsa looked worriedly to the storm. "If you would just bring back the summer," he added.

"I can't," she said. "You have to tell them to let me go."

"I will do what I can," replied Hans, before leaving Elsa alone in her cell.

Meanwhile, Sven was speeding towards Arendelle,
with Kristoff and Anna on his back. "Just hang in
there," Kristoff said to Anna. It was clear to him that
she was getting weaker.

At the castle gates, he passed her to two royal servants. "You poor girl, let's get you inside," said one of them.

"Get her warm and find Prince Hans," said Kristoff. "Make sure she's safe," he added. Feeling there was nothing more he could do, Kristoff left Arendelle.

Anna was taken to a room with a warm fire and left with Hans. She explained to him what he had to do. But he refused. "Oh, Anna," he said, sneering. "If only there was someone out there who loved you."

As Anna looked on helplessly, Hans put out the fire. He told Anna that he only pretended to love her so he could take over Arendelle. All he had to do now was get rid of Elsa. "Anna will return, and the kingdom will be mine," he said.

Locking Anna in the room and leaving her to die, Hans met with
the others in the castle. Everyone looked to him for guidance
regarding what to do with Elsa. "With a heavy heart," said Hans,
"I charge Queen Elsa with treason and sentence her to death."

As they rushed to Elsa's cell, the queen overheard what they were planning and so, using her powers, she managed to break open her shackles and blast a hole in the wall. She had to get away from Arendelle for the good of everyone.

Hans and the guards burst in moments later, but they were too late. Elsa had escaped.

As Anna sat alone, she suddenly heard the locked door open. It was Olaf! He'd managed to unlock the door with his carrot nose!

As Olaf relit the fire, Anna explained what Hans had done. The little snowman suggested that a kiss from Kristoff might help. "Kristoff loves me?" asked Anna, before quickly adding, "Olaf, you're melting."

"Some people are worth melting for," he replied.

Just then, the window blew open. As Olaf went to close it, he noticed something. Using an icicle as a telescope, he looked into the distance. "It's Kristoff and Sven!" cried Olaf. "They're coming back this way."

There was still a chance to save Anna with a true love's kiss!

Olaf helped Anna outside, where she spotted Kristoff across the frozen fjord. There was just enough time to reach him before she froze solid.

However, she saw something else. Hans had caught up with Elsa and was about to strike her with his sword!

Anna sprinted as fast as she could to protect her sister and, with her remaining strength, managed to get between Elsa and Hans just as his sword came swinging down.

Anna's body froze to solid ice and, as the sword made contact with her, the blade shattered. The shock wave threw Hans off his feet and knocked him out.

"Anna!" cried Elsa, throwing her arms around her
sister. As tears fell from Elsa's cheeks, something
amazing happened. Anna began to thaw!
"You sacrificed yourself for me," said Elsa.

"I love you" replied Anna.

"An act of true love will thaw a frozen heart,"
said Olaf, realising what had happened.

With Anna saved, and Elsa realising love could bring back summer, she raised her arms and the snow melted away. With summer restored to Arendelle, life returned to normal, only this time the castle gates were open for good!

Elsa then created a special snow cloud for Olaf so he could enjoy the summer, and Kristoff and Anna finally kissed. The evil Hans was also banished from the kingdom, never to return.

To celebrate, Queen Elsa created an ice-skating rink
in the castle and invited the whole kingdom. At long
last, the kingdom of Arendelle was a happy place
once more.

THE END

COLLECT THEM ALL!

With 7 more exciting titles to choose from, you'll want to complete your Storytime Collection!

How far will a father go for his son?

Will Rapunzel learn who she truly is?

Will Moana be able to save the ocean?

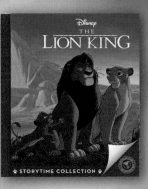

Will Simba ever become king?

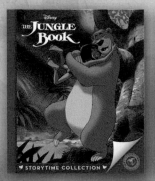

Will Mowgli defeat Shere Khan?

Will the Incredibles save the day?

Will Belle be able to break the curse?